Lapin Plays Possum

Trickster Tales from the Louisiana Bayou

Adapted by Sharon Arms Doucet
Pictures by Scott Cook

Melanie Kroupa Books
Farrar, Straus and Giroux • New York

GLOSSARY

bayou (BY yoo): wide, slow-moving stream

bien bon (bee yah BOH): good, great

bonsoir (boh SWAR): good evening

bouki (boo KEE): hyena in the Wolof language of Africa

commencé (coh moh SAY): just begun

compère (comb PARE): comrade, brother

derrière (dare ee AIR): behind

do-do (doh DOH): night-night

gumbo (GUM boh): a thick stew with a flour and oil base

hein (ehn, but leave off the *N*): what did you say?

lapin (lah PAN, but leave off the *N*): rabbit

Mardi Gras (mahr dee GRAH): Fat Tuesday, a day of masked revelry before Lent

merci beaucoup (mare SEE boh COO): thank you very much

moi (mwah): me

moitié (mwah T'YAY): half; halfway

mon ami (mon nah MEE): my friend

parrain (pah RAN, without the *N*): godfather

picayune (pick ee YOON): a coin with little value; also anything small or trivial

quoi ça dit? (kwah sah DEE): what's going on?

sauce piquante (sahs pee KAHNT): a spicy stew with a tomato base

'tee mademoiselle (tee mahd mwah ZEL): little lady

'Tee Tar Bébé (tee tar bay BAY): Little Tar Baby

tout fini (too fee NEE): all gone

Down by the boggy bayous of Louisiana lived critters of all shapes and sizes. Some were big as bullies, and others were puny as a picayune penny. Some were as sharp as a bee's stinger, and others were duller than a wooden nickel. There were those that came into the world with a silver spoon to suck on, while others got nothing but a cypress splinter.

Take Compère Bouki, for instance. He cast a shadow big as a barnyard. He owned a farming field full of Delta soil so rich that if you planted a penny at sunrise, you could pick a dollar before sundown. But as for smarts, he must have been hiding behind the barn door when they were passed out.

Now Compère Lapin, on the other hand, wasn't but knee-high to a blackberry bush, and his cupboards were so bare he could stretch himself out and sleep in them. He could find more ways to get out of work than there are fleas on a possum. But Lapin, him, he'd got an extra helping of smarts. And so things didn't always turn out as you might expect.

One summer Bouki got overambitious when he planted his cotton field. There was so much plowing and planting and tending and hoeing to be done in that hot Louisiana sun that, by harvesttime, he was so pooped he could barely blink an eye. As the cotton bolls started popping out around him like firecrackers on New Year's Eve, he knew he had to get himself some help.

Now Lapin, who'd spent the whole summer lollygagging in the shade of the sassafras tree, had a way of showing up at times like these. And Compère Bouki was so desperate that, against his better judgment, he decided to ask that half-pint hare for help.

"Say, Lapin," he asked, "what would you take to help me harvest this cotton crop?"

Lapin shaded his eyes and surveyed the cotton field that glimmered like a snowdrift all the way to the bayou. Knowing he could hoodwink Bouki quicker than he could sneeze, he said, "Whew, that's a heap of cotton. I'd have to get at least an eighth of it to make it worth my slaving in the hot sun."

Bouki scratched his ear. He'd never been very good at figuring. "I'll give you one-fourth," he said, being as four was littler than eight.

Lapin's ears pricked up as he followed Bouki's line of thinking. "You drive a hard bargain, Bouki," he said. "But I wouldn't want to take advantage of you. I suppose I could do it for a third."

"Half," said Bouki, thinking that half had a two in it, and that was smaller than a three.

"Deal," said Lapin, hiding a grin.

"*Bien bon*," said Bouki, figuring he'd gotten the best of the bargain. "Here's you a sack, and here's me a sack. Let's get to work."

Now Lapin couldn't resist playing tricks on Bouki any more than he could turn down a piece of King Cake on Mardi Gras. "I can't wait to get to work," he said sweetly. "But looks to me like we'll be needing something to celebrate with at the end of the harvest. What say we treat ourselves to a barrel of rum cake?"

"Oh, all right," grumbled Bouki. He loved nothing better than rum cake himself. "Go ahead and get some butter to go with it."

So Lapin hopped off to the store and charged a nice fat barrel of sweet rum cake to Bouki's account. (And a nice fat barrel of butter, too.) He stashed them under the cool bank of the bayou so the butter wouldn't melt in the sun.

Then they set to picking cotton.

Bouki went *pick, pick, pick* and *pluck, pluck, pluck*. But Lapin went *pick . . . pluck . . . pick . . . pluck*. His sack had barely begun to bulge before he pricked up his elongated ears and called, *"Hein?* What's that you say?"

"What?" said Bouki from the next row.

"There it is again. One of my sisters is calling me to a baptism. She wants me to be the godfather to her baby and help name the little thing."

"I didn't hear nothing," said Bouki.

"Course you didn't. That's 'cause you got such puny ears," said Lapin.

"Go on, then," growled Compère Bouki. "I don't suppose you can turn down an invitation to be a *parrain*."

So Lapin dropped his sack and hightailed it out of the field. But he didn't go to any baptism. No, he circled around and headed straight for the bayou and that barrel of butter. Naturally, he had to have something to spread it on, so he cut himself a thick slice of rum cake, too. Oh, that butter was so smooth, so creamy, that cake so sweet and spicy, that he just had to have another slice. And another after that.

Finally, when his belly couldn't hold another bite, he decided it was time to get back to the cotton picking.

Bouki's sack was nearly full by then, but there was plenty left to pick. "About time you got back," he said. "What'd they name the baby?"

"Oh, uh, they named it *Commençé*," said Lapin.

Bouki shook his shaggy head. "What're folks thinking, naming a baby 'Just Begun'?"

Lapin shrugged and got to picking. *Pick . . . Pluck . . . Pick . . . Pluck.*

'Long about noon, Lapin's sack was still as empty as a hatched egg. And even though his belly was stuffed fuller than a squirrel's cheeks, all that cake and all that butter kept dancing through his mind.

So he lifted his head and cocked his ear. "Coming!" he called out into thin air.

"Who dat?" said Bouki, shading his eyes from the sun.

Lapin sighed. "This time it's my little brother calling. I got to be god-father again."

"Ain't they got enough of you rabbits already?" Bouki sighed. "Well, go on, then." And he went back to picking.

Lapin skedaddled over to the bayou, pulled up the barrels, and had himself a little noontime snack. Well, it was bigger than little. In fact, it was downright humongous.

When he trudged on back to the field, Bouki was sweating over his second sack of cotton. "What'd they name the baby this time?" he grumbled. "Halfway?"

"How did you guess?" said Lapin. "*Moitié* it is."

Compère Bouki just shook his head and said, "What next?" Compère Lapin went back to picking cotton, working slower than a slug on Sunday.

The sun had warmed things up something fierce by the time three o'clock rolled around. And sure enough, Lapin perked up his ears again and called out, "I'll be there shortly."

"Not another baptism?" snapped Compère Bouki.

"If you can't hear them calling me, you ought to get your ears checked."

Bouki surveyed all the cotton they had left to pick, but by then he was too tired to argue, so he waved Lapin on off.

This time Compère Lapin scraped the bottom of the butter barrel with the last crumbs of the rum cake. His belly was so full he could barely waddle on back to the cotton field.

"They named it *Tout Fini*," Lapin told Bouki with a glint in his eye. " 'All Done,' 'cause I ain't going to be *parrain* to no more babies!"

Come quitting time, Compère Bouki dragged sack after sack out of the field, while Lapin had a few measly clumps of cotton floating in the bottom of his. Bouki limped toward the bayou, his mouth watering. "The only thing that kept me going all day," he groaned, "was the thought of all that sweet rum cake and all that cool, creamy butter."

But when he hoisted the barrels up from the bank of that bayou, they were emptier than the church basket come the day after Christmas.

Bouki swung a suspicious look at Lapin, and pulled himself up till he towered over him. "Why, you little scoundrel—"

"*Moi?*" said Lapin, acting innocent as a newborn baby.

"Wait'll I get my hands on that puny little neck of yours . . ." But just then Bouki's mouth opened in a barrel-sized yawn, and his eyelids clamped shut. And he fell into a standing-up, tuckered-out sleep.

All that rich food and hard labor had made Lapin drowsy, too. So, putting a little distance between himself and Bouki, he lay down and dozed off as well.

But the late afternoon sun blazed down on Lapin's overstuffed belly, and all that butter inside of it began to melt. He woke up in an oily puddle big as the Gulf of Mexico.

"Uh-oh," said Lapin, scampering off to the bayou to clean himself up.

Then, when he saw Bouki still asleep in his tracks, a trick popped into Lapin's head like a popcorn kernel in a frying pan.

He commenced to pushing and shoving on Bouki's broad backside till Bouki fell right smack dollop into that puddle of butter. Then Lapin smeared that oily mess all over Bouki's mouth and paws till he was greasier than a politician's palm.

Shaking him awake, Lapin cried, "Why, Bouki, just look at you! *You're* the one that ate the butter while I was off at the baptisms!"

Bouki blinked and licked his lips. "I-I didn't do it, I swear, Lapin."

"A likely story," said Lapin. "Here you sit in a whole puddle of evidence."

"I surely don't recollect it," said Bouki, "unless sunstroke put me outta my head."

"Humph," said Lapin. "A deal's a deal. You owe me half a barrel of butter and half a barrel of rum cake, too."

Compère Bouki couldn't do nothing but scratch his greasy old head.

So that's how that rascal Lapin got to have his butter and his rum cake, not once, but twice. Not to mention one-half of Bouki's cotton crop.

It just goes to show, there's more than one way to crop a cotton field.
Especially for a picayunish prankster like Compère Lapin.

Lapin Plays Possum

Compère Bouki never was sure whether or not he'd eaten that barrel of cake and that barrel of butter. But he did know that somehow Compère Lapin had got half of a good crop without doing but a speck of work. And that got his dander up.

So when Lapin showed up come planting time talking about making another deal, Bouki said, "No way, no how. You get your *derrière* to work on your own crop." Then he remembered a scraggly patch of land way back by the bayou that he never got around to working. "I tell you what I could do, though—I could rent you a field."

"For how much?" asked Lapin.

Bouki thought the time was ripe to even the score with Lapin. So, with a sly grin, he said, "We'd share the crop fair and square—I'd get the top of the plant, and you'd get all the rest." He could just see himself collecting sack after sack of cotton while Lapin got nothing but roots and stems.

Lapin shuffled his feet and scratched his head. Finally he said, "You drive a heap of a hard bargain, Bouki. But a feller's got to make a living—I guess you got yourself a deal."

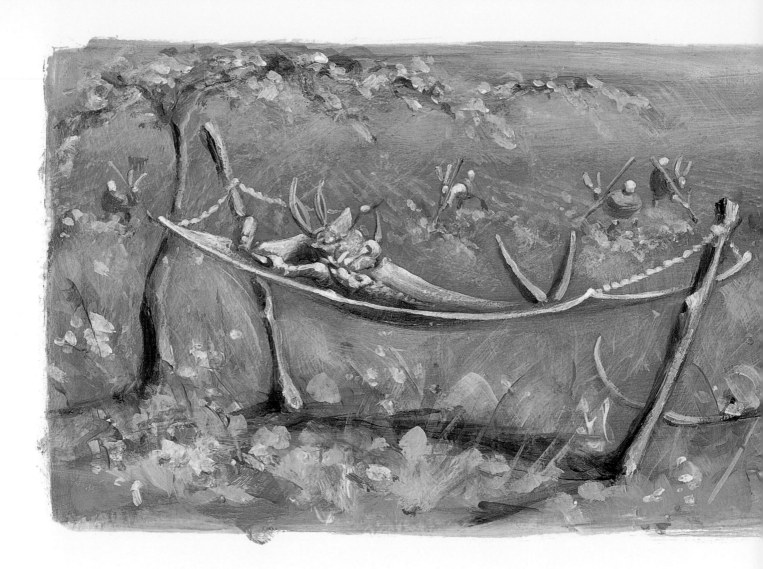

So next summer, come cropping time, Bouki trekked off to the back field ready to collect all of Lapin's cotton. To his surprise, he found that rabbit stretched out under a mimosa tree, drinking a mint julep and over-seeing all his cousins and nieces and nephews as they hoed the field. And there, as far as the eye could see, stretched sweet potato vines greener than ten-dollar bills and thicker than a passel of lawyers in cahoots.

"I'm right glad you came by," said Compère Lapin, chewing on a mint leaf. "Soon as you collect your vines I'll get to digging my sweet 'taters."

"Sweet potatoes!" roared Bouki. "Why, you scrawny, slippery little scoundrel. Those vines don't amount to nothing but a compost heap!" He stormed off, blowing steam like a locomotive engine. And that left Lapin to collect a cellar full of plump sweet potatoes that kept him fat and sassy till the buzzing of the spring bees.

Next year, Compère Bouki was determined not to get hornswoggled by Compère Lapin. So when that rabbit came by to talk about renting the field again, Bouki said, "No, sirree. This is *my* land, and you ain't cheating me twice."

"Why, Compère Bouki, I never cheated you," said Lapin. "You made the deal yourself. I only gave you what you wanted."

"Well, I ain't no fool. I'll rent you that field, but this time, *you* take the tops, and I get the rest."

Lapin looked all droopy. "You're a hard straw boss, I guarantee. But it's a deal."

Come harvesttime, Bouki couldn't wait to get the best of Lapin, along with all those plump sweet potatoes. But when he looked out over Lapin's field, he couldn't believe his eyeballs. There was clump after plump clump of rice waving in the bayou breeze.

"I'm right glad to see you," said Lapin. "I done harvested the grain heads off my rice crop. Now you can haul off your rice straw and your roots."

"Straw and roots!" sputtered Bouki, heading home empty-handed. But, like a gambler who's got to play just one more hand of poker, he was sure he could figure out a way to win.

By planting time, he thought he had a plan all worked out.

"This time," he said, looming over Lapin like a mule over a mouse, "you can rent my field if you give me both the tops *and* the bottoms."

"But, Bouki," said Lapin, "that don't leave nothing for poor little old me."

"Why, you can have the middles," said Bouki with a chuckle, figuring he'd bested Lapin for sure this time.

"I don't see how you expect me to live on that. But I declare, you got me over a barrel." Lapin sighed as they shook on the deal.

Come harvesttime, Bouki took his wagon out to the field to see whether Lapin had grown him sweet potatoes or rice.

"You're just in time, neighbor," said Lapin from atop a loaded wagon. "We just finished picking all that good-for-nothing corn off the middles of the plants. I left you just what you wanted—some nice fat tassels and some big strong roots."

Tassels and roots! Well, that did it. Bouki vowed to have nothing to do with Lapin, not ever again. So the next year, Bouki farmed his land all by his lonesome. He plowed and he planted, he weeded and he hoed. Every once in a while, Lapin would drop by to see how the work was going. "Need some help?" he'd ask.

"Not from *you*," Bouki answered. When the crop was ready, he picked that cotton all by himself, loaded his cart, and headed to town.

His crop fetched a pretty price, and all that money was burning a hole in Bouki's pocket just about the time that hunger started knocking on his belly. So he bought himself a steaming kettle of seafood gumbo, and another of sweet bread pudding. Taking a little taste of each just to tide him over till he got home, he loaded his loot onto the cart and took off down the road.

Meanwhile, never let it be said that Lapin heard opportunity knock without answering the door. He'd spent the afternoon lollygagging in the shade by the side of the road, all the while keeping one ear pressed to the ground. When he heard Bouki's cartwheels coming from town, and smelled that gumbo and bread pudding, he hauled himself out into the middle of the road, plopped himself down, and held his breath till he looked deader than a possum playing possum.

"Whoa," said Bouki to his mule. "It looks like a rabbit done bit the dust. It's a good thing I got plenty o' provisions here, or I might've picked up that fat ole thing for supper, and who knows how long it's been a-laying there." He clucked to the mule and rode on.

Well, as soon as Bouki was out of sight, Lapin jumped up, hightailed it around through the woods, and laid himself down in the road again, just as Bouki was coming around the bend. The smell of all that food was teasing his taste buds, but he held his breath and made like he was dead.

"Whoa!" said Bouki to his mule. "Another rabbit's expired. They must all be dying of eternal laziness. Serves 'em right." He clucked to his mule and rode on.

Well, guess what, Lapin got up and raced pell-mell through the woods, threw himself down on the ground, and imitated a dead doornail.

"Whoa!" said Bouki when he saw him. He scratched his head. "Durned if that don't beat all. Now I just can't resist taking this nice fat one home with me. I'll make me a rabbit *sauce piquante* for sure." He got down, picked up that possum-playing rabbit, and tossed him into the back of the cart.

Then Bouki scratched his head. "Come to think of it, seems to me that first rabbit I passed bore a strong resemblance to Compère Lapin. I don't care if I've already got more food than a horse has flies—I'm going to run back and get that scoundrel!"

As soon as Bouki was out of sight, Lapin raised himself up from the dead and grabbed the reins of the cart, ready to make off with all that gumbo and all that bread pudding. But because it was his nature, he thought up something better.

He plucked some hair from that mule's tail and ran over to a big pothole in the road. Then, just like he was planting a rosebush, he stuck the mule hair down into the hole and pulled up a little dirt around it. He skedaddled back to the cart, gave a giddy-up to the mule, and drove on home.

After Compère Lapin had consumed a king-size bowl of gumbo, he had a king-size serving of sweet bread pudding. He stashed the kettles in his cellar, hid the mule and cart in the barn, and headed back up the road to see how Compère Bouki was getting along.

There was Bouki, waist-deep in a fresh excavation and working a shovel like crazy.

"Say there, Compère Bouki," said Lapin, "what in tarnation are you doing?"

At the sound of Lapin's voice, Bouki shot out of that hole like a pea out of a peashooter. "Y-you're alive!" he sputtered. "But I thought—"

"What's the matter, *mon ami?*" said Lapin. "You look like you've seen a ghost."

Bouki's knees gave out from under him, and he patted his pounding heart. "I-I dropped something up the road a ways," he panted, "and when I went back to get it, my mule and cart musta fell in this here pothole. I got to dig 'em out afore that mule smothers to death." He reached out to touch Lapin. "You're sure enough alive, ain't you?"

"Alive and kicking," said Lapin. "What makes you think your mule fell in that hole?"

"Because his tail's sticking out of it, of course!"

Compère Lapin sat down to enjoy the goings-on until Compère Bouki finally gave up. Then, feeling kindly, he invited Bouki home for dinner.

By then Bouki's belly was so empty that he followed Lapin home, and slurped down a bowl of the thick, spicy soup. "I do declare, Lapin," he said, wiping his mouth, "this is almost as good as the gumbo that fell down that pothole. It's right kindly of you to share it with me."

Compère Lapin helped himself to another bowl so Bouki wouldn't have to eat alone. "Why, think nothing of it." He grinned. "I'm just being neighborly."

Then he rubbed his bulging belly, wondering what Bouki would provide for him next.

Lapin Tangles with 'Tee Tar Bébé

One day Compère Bouki spied Compère Lapin driving a wagon and mule looking suspiciously like the ones that fell down the pothole. That's when he realized that, once again, he'd been had by that runt of a rabbit. And from that day on, Bouki resolved to find a way to turn the tables on Lapin.

It was July in south Louisiana, and hotter than Cajun pepper sauce. It hadn't rained a drop since Mardi Gras. The leaves shriveled, the bayous parched, and the air shimmered like swamp fire in the sizzling heat.

Compère Lapin lay in the shade, swatting at flies and trying not to let his tongue hang out. Suddenly he pricked up his long and lanky ears. *Scritch, scratch, thump,* he heard from the other side of the bamboo thicket.

He crawled through the underbrush to see what was going on, and came upon Compère Bouki dredging out a deep hole. "I'm so thirsty," Bouki was muttering, "I could cry just so's I could drink my own tears."

"*Quoi ça dit,* Bouki?" said Lapin. "You lost yourself another mule?"

Bouki looked up with a scowl. "Leave me alone, Lapin. I'm digging myself a well."

Compère Lapin wasn't about to let on that he was a mite thirsty himself. "What you need a well for?" he said. "Me, I get plenty o' water from the morning dew. And if that don't do it, I just digs me a cocklebur root to chew on. You ought to give it a try."

"I ain't sucking on no cocklebur root," said Bouki. "But I got to have a drink of water before I shrivel up like a dried shrimp."

Scritch, scratch, thump, went his shovel. "And don't think you'll get a single drop when I hit water!"

Bouki shoveled and he scooped, he grunted and he groaned. But Lapin, he just lolled around in the shade, grinning like he was watching the Saturday afternoon picture show.

Compère Bouki kept on digging. It wasn't till 'long about sundown that he cried "Pay dirt!" from the bottom of the hole. And sure enough, he'd struck a trickle of water.

Compère Lapin peeked over the edge of the well, his mouth watering at the tinkling of that liquid refreshment.

Bouki slurped noisily. "It's too bad you ain't thirsty, Lapin," he called up, " 'cause this water's sweeter'n honeysuckle juice!"

Lapin swallowed hard, then stuck his nose up in the air. "I don't care for any, *merci beaucoup,*" he said.

"Well, see that it stays that way," said Bouki, climbing out. " 'Cause if you so much as sniff at a single drop, I'll have you for supper this very night—and I don't mean for company!" He waited till Lapin had sashayed off, then he went home to get some sleep.

Now Bouki should've known that as soon as he told that rogue of a rabbit not to do something, that was the very thing he made up his mind to do. No sooner was the moon up than Lapin crept back and set himself down on the edge of the well. By then the hole had filled itself to the top, and all he had to do was to lean over and lap up that sweet water.

Before long, Lapin's gullet was wetter than a frog's toenails. But he thought how, come daylight, the sun would heat things up, and he'd be drier than a desert dust devil again. So he fetched himself a bunch of calabash gourds, filled them from the well, and lugged them on home. That way he'd never even have to get out of bed when he got thirsty, but could nap the livelong day.

Early next morning, Compère Bouki waltzed himself over to the well. He knelt down, leaned over with his parched lips all puckered out—and nearly fell down the empty hole. It was dry as dust, except for a sad little puddle way down at the bottom.

"Hmm," he said, scratching his head. "Either there's a leak in my well, or somebody stole my water." Sure enough, the grass was all trampled down, and Lapin was nowhere in sight.

As the well filled up again, Bouki took to standing guard over it like it was Napoleon's tomb. But by nightfall he was so hot and tuckered out that he nodded off. Lapin, waking up from his hard day's sleep, heard Bouki snoring like the steam engine on yesterday's train. He tippy-toed right past him and took a long, lazy drink. Then he filled his calabash gourds and went on home.

This went on until one day Bouki had had enough. "This very night," he said to himself, "I'm gonna catch the varmint that's stealing my water. And I'll lay ten to one that it turns out to be a rabbit!"

So Bouki fetched himself some soft, sticky coal tar. Recollecting Lapin's fondness for the ladies, he patted and plumped that gooey glop till he'd fashioned a female figure near the well.

"All right, 'Tee Tar Bébé," he said. "You stand guard here, and we'll see what we can ambush." Then he stole into the bushes to watch. But before long, being as it was past his bedtime, his eyelids got heavier than a bale of cotton, and he drifted off to *do-do* land.

Well, it wasn't long before Compère Lapin came skipping along with his empty calabashes and a powerful thirst. In the pale light of the moon, he saw somebody who wasn't Bouki sitting right there beside the well.

Lapin ducked into the blackberry bushes. By and by, when he made out that it was a female somebody, he stepped out into the moonlight like a mouse to a trap. "Yoo-hoo! *Bonsoir, 'tee mademoiselle!*"

The 'Tee Tar Bébé didn't answer.

Lapin snuck a little closer. "Aw, no need to be shy."

'Tee Tar Bébé kept quiet.

Lapin strutted right up beside her. "How 'bout giving us a kiss, *'tee mademoiselle?*" And he closed his eyes, puckered his lips, and leaned in for a big fat smooch.

Well, 'Tee Tar Bébé grabbed him by the kisser and wouldn't let go.

"That's enough," mumbled Lapin around a mouthful of tar. "Let me come up for air, won't you?"

Lapin tried to push away with his right hand. But 'Tee Tar Bébé caught hold of it, too. "I swear, you hug like a puddle of quicksand," said Lapin. He pushed with his left hand, and it stuck, too.

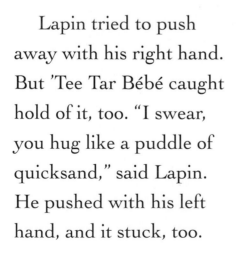

"Hey, take it easy," cried Lapin, trying to get a toehold with his right foot. Then his left. But they both stuck faster than a fat fist in a cookie jar.

He was snared but good.

And that's when Lapin realized he'd been had by old Compère Bouki.

There he stayed, with nothing to think about but the rum cake and the butter, the sweet potatoes, rice, and corn, the gumbo and the bread pudding, and all the calabash gourds of water he'd weaseled out of Bouki. And as he shivered through that long and lonesome night, he *almost* wished he'd never done any of those deeds.

Next morning, the sun woke Bouki. When he spied Lapin all stuck in that coal tar, he danced a gleeful jig. "I knowed it was you what's been stealing my water. After all this time, I caught you at last! And now I'm going to hang you from the tippy-top of that chinaball tree."

Lapin gulped. His head might've been stuck in the tar, but his smarts were still running loose. "Hang me from the chinaball tree, I don't care," he said. "But whatever you do, don't throw me in that blackberry patch."

"Why not?" said Bouki.

" 'Cause my poor little hide's too tender for those sharp, spiky thorns."

"Come to think on it," said Bouki, "that tree is mighty tall to climb. Maybe I'll build a bonfire and have me some barbecued rabbit."

"Roast me in the fire, hang me from the highest tree," Lapin said, his voice a-trembling. "Just don't throw me in those blackberry briers."

"It is right hot to build a fire. Maybe I'll drown you in my well. That'd serve you right!"

"Drown me, hang me, barbecue me in the fire," said Lapin. "But those blackberry briers are my worstest nightmare come true."

"Blackberry briers, huh?" said Bouki. "That does sound like the fastestest way to put an end to you. And if you hates them so bad, that's just what I'm gonna do."

So Compère Bouki plucked Lapin from 'Tee Tar Bébé's embrace, wound up his pitching arm once, twice, three times, and flung him *ka-CHUNK* into the matted tangle of blackberry vines.

Then he cocked his ears and listened for Compère Lapin to start moaning and groaning in those sticker bushes.

He heard a little rustling. He heard a little brustling. But he heard no moaning and no groaning.

He leaned farther into the briers to see what could've happened.

Just then Lapin stuck out his head. He was grinning from long ear to long ear.

"Thank you so kindly for turning me loose," said Lapin sweetly.

"Turning you loose?" said Bouki, dumbfounded.

"Why yes, *mon ami*—don't you know those stickers skim right off a rabbit's fur? Fact is, you delivered me to the very brier patch where my dear old mama brought me into the world."

Compère Bouki made a mighty lunge after him. But those stickery vines didn't skim right off *his* fur; in fact, they latched on like a flea on a catahoula hound.

The more Bouki fought, the more tangled up
he got, until he was snared like a stinkbug
in a spider web. Compère Lapin
just grinned and lay down
in the middle of the
briers to catch up
on his sleep.

Which all just goes to show you that size ain't everything in this world. It's what you do with what you got that matters.

If you should ever catch up to Compère Lapin, just ask him.

Author's Note

The trickster Compère Lapin and his sidekick, Compère Bouki, have been pestering each other since before they left their native soil of western Africa over two centuries ago. In the early 1700s, they were brought to North America by the African men and women who were captured and sold into slavery. They quarreled all the way to French-speaking Louisiana, where folks have been telling their stories around the hearth and on the porch ever since, in both the black Creole and the white Cajun communities.

Lapin's famous cousin ended up on the East Coast and is known to all as Brer Rabbit. Bouki started life in Africa as a hyena. But since hyenas tend to be scarce in Louisiana, he has evolved into a vague dog-wolf character, always large on size but short on brains.

The author has taken liberties in the recounting and recombining of the tales. Compère Lapin has grinned over her shoulder the whole way.

To my Ezra, who never runs out of tricks to make me smile,
and to the memory of Mary Frances Doucet,
who made the best rum cake in the world
—S.A.D.

For Retta
—S.C.

Text copyright © 2002 by Sharon Arms Doucet
Illustrations copyright © 2002 by Scott Cook
All rights reserved
Distributed in Canada by Douglas & McIntyre Ltd.
Color separations by Bright Arts (H.K.) Ltd.
Printed and bound in Hong Kong by South China Printing Company (1988) Ltd.
Book design by Jennifer Browne
First edition, 2002
1   3   5   7   9   10   8   6   4   2

Library of Congress Cataloging-in-Publication Data

Doucet, Sharon Arms.
    Lapin plays possum : trickster tales from the Louisiana Bayou / adapted by Sharon
Arms Doucet ; pictures by Scott Cook.— 1st ed.
        p. cm.
    Summary: In a series of incidents, the rascal Lapin finds many different ways to outwit
Compère Bouki.
    ISBN 0-374-34328-4
    1. Tales—Louisiana. [1. Folklore—Louisiana.] I. Cook, Scott, ill. II. Title.
PZ8.1.D75 Lap 2002
398.2'09763'02—dc21

                                                                        2001029387